HOOEY ♥ HIGGINS
and the
CHRISTMAS CRASH

For Maggie Earley-Urquhart
S.V.

For Jacky Paynter, for all your
hard work and cheerful support
E.D.

HOOEY HIGGINS
and the
CHRISTMAS CRASH

STEVE VOAKE
illustrated by Emma Dodson

WALKER
BOOKS

First published 2014 by Walker Books Ltd
87 Vauxhall Walk, London SE11 5HJ

2 4 6 8 10 9 7 5 3 1

Text © 2014 Steve Voake
Illustrations © 2014 Emma Dodson

The right of Steve Voake and Emma Dodson to be identified as author and illustrator respectively of this work has been asserted by them in accordance with the Copyright, Designs and Patents Act 1988

This book has been typeset in StempelSchneidler and EDodson

Printed and bound in Great Britain
by Clays Ltd, St Ives plc

British Library Cataloguing in Publication Data:
a catalogue record for this book is available from the British Library

ISBN 978-1-4063-4332-8

www.walker.co.uk

CONTENTS

Mr Danson

Frank and Freddie
Frinton

Sarah-Jane
Silverton

Twig

Hooey

CHRISTMAS CRASH

"Snow, snow, snow," sang Twig, "I never want it to go. Ice, ice, ice, is nearly just as nice."

"Bash the babbies!" shouted Basbo. "Bash the babbies!"

"Are those two feeling all right?" asked Samantha as they climbed to the top of the hill behind Shrimpton-on-Sea. Thick snowflakes drifted from the sky, covering the fields in a blanket of white.

"They're practising for the **Christmas play**," said Hooey. "Basbo's King Herod and Twig's one of the singing sheep. What are you?"

"Angel Gabriel."

"I thought he was a bloke."

"The Angel Gabriel is not a 'bloke', Hooey. The Angel Gabriel is a beautiful vision who appears on a hillside."

"Wearing a ski suit from Topshop?"

"I'm off duty at the moment," said Samantha. "**Who's playing Mary?**"

"Sarah Jane Silverton."

"You're joking," said Samantha. "She looks awful in blue." "Tell me about it," said Yasmin. "I auditioned wearing Plumpy-Lips lipstick and sparkly blue eyeshadow, but Miss Troutson just laughed and gave me the part of the barmaid."

"Maybe you could work your way up to landlady," said Samantha. "Like that woman off *Eastenders*."

"...and play in it, and play in it,
and play in it, and play in it,"
Twig sang, skipping around at the
top of the hill.
"And then I
want to stay in it,
to stay in it,
to stay in it..."

There was a loud **clang** and Twig toppled sideways as if he had been shot.

Behind him, Basbo held a tin tray with a dent in it. "**Bash the babbies!**" he shouted. "**Bash the babbies!**"

Twig sat up and rubbed his head. "I'm not a babby. I'm a sheep."

"Perhaps you're a babby sheep," said Wayne. "One of them lamby things."

"I izz killin' lambies too," said Basbo. "Speshully va noisy ones."

"Basbo takes his acting very seriously," whispered Hooey.

Basbo sat on his tin tray, shouted

Bash the babbies!

and launched himself down the slope.

"Bye," said Twig as Basbo flew down the hill like a bullock on a bobsleigh. "Don't crash, will you?"

> **And we have ... lift-off!**

said Hooey
as Basbo hit a bump
and shot into the air like a
small aeroplane made from bones,
beef and an easy-clean tracksuit.
As the tin tray separated from
Basbo's bottom, Hooey was

impressed by the way he somehow managed to turn around in the air in an attempt to catch it. But just as his fingers closed around the edge, he hit the ground, cartwheeled over the water trough and landed in a thorn bush, where the tray finally caught up with him and bonked him on the head.

"Ooh," said Samantha,

that's gotta hurt.

"My turn now!" said Twig, pulling a black bin bag from his pocket.

"Hang on, y'doughnut," said Samantha. "Didn't you see what happened to Basbo?"

Twig grinned. "Are you worried about me, Samantha?"

"Yes," said Samantha. "But only because you haven't got any brains."

Twig turned to Hooey and put his thumbs up. "Samantha's worried about me," he said.

"Best give her something to worry about then," said Hooey. He put his feet on the plank of wood he'd found at the back of his garage and wrapped the string around his trainers. The end of the plank was still splintered where he'd sawn the edges off, but apart from that it looked pretty good, like the pointy end of a battleship.

Stand well back, people,

he said. "This Shrimpton Snowboard only works at speeds over a billion miles per hour."

"It'll need to if it's going to catch *us*," said Yasmin. "Ready, Samantha?"

"Ready," said Samantha. Both girls were strapped to sporty-looking skis.

See you at the bottom, losers!

The girls
set off down
the hill and
Hooey jumped
forward, leaning
into the wind. Having
spent the previous evening
melting candles onto the
bottom of his snowboard he'd
noticed that the results were
a bit lumpy, so he'd rubbed a tin
of furniture polish over the top and
added a few squirts of washing-up liquid
for extra slippiness. He felt as if he was
gliding effortlessly across the surface of the
snow, flying over bumps and bobbles as the
wind blew his hair back and brought tears to
his eyes. Crouching lower, he fixed his eyes
on the bottom of the hill and watched the
fields turn to a blur.

"I beat you!" he shouted, as he shot past the girls like a silver bullet.

He bounced off the side of the water trough and shot into the air, the two halves of his broken snowboard flying next to him like little geese on their way to sunnier shores.

Hooey flapped his arms, but gravity was against him. As he fell from the sky, Basbo suddenly appeared from the thorn bush. Hooey thumped into his arms with a startled yelp. Basbo grunted but stayed on his feet, stumbling from the bushes with Hooey clutched firmly against his chest.

Hooey smiled awkwardly.

"Hello," he said. "Do you come here often?"

Before Basbo could answer, Yasmin and Samantha arrived with a swish of skis.

Samantha looked at Hooey in Basbo's arms and raised an eyebrow. "If I'd known you two were getting married," she said, "I'd have got here earlier."

"Noggen marreed," said Basbo, dropping Hooey in the snow.

"No, we most certainly are *not*," said Hooey, brushing snow from his hair. "Not if that's the way you treat a lady."

23

There was a distant scream and everyone turned to see Twig and Wayne careering down the hill, trying to steer their bin bag with two bits of string.

Go left!

shouted Wayne, clinging onto Twig's ears. "Go left! Go left!"

"I'm trying to go left!" Twig yelled back. He jerked his hands up and there was a faint snapping sound.

"Uhh," said Basbo. "Iss brokey-busted."

"Code Red!" shouted Twig as they hit a bump and left the ground, still huddled together in a sitting position as if they were driving an invisible car. "String malfunction!"

"Go left!" screamed Wayne. "GO LEFT! GO LEFT!"

Twig held up the piece of string to show Wayne that going left was not an option. Then the tips of his trainers struck the water trough and he flipped forwards into it, splintering the ice with his face. Wayne kept travelling until he hit the ground with a whump, skidded under the gate and disappeared into a snowdrift.

"Man overboard!" spluttered Twig, clawing at the sides of the water trough. "Launch the lifeboats!"

Basbo grabbed him by the ankle and spun him around his head.

Issa wool-wash time!

he shouted.

"Spin the sheep-boy rownunn round!"

"I really don't think—" said Samantha, but before she could finish, Twig's foot slipped out of his trainer and he shot over the gate into the snowdrift.

Basbo stared at the empty trainer in his hand, then up at the sky.  **"Sheep-boy gone spacey-bam,"** he said.

Wayne stuck his head out of the drift and spat out a mouthful of snow. "Anyone seen Twig?" he asked.

"Here he is," said Twig, popping his head out next to him.

"Sheepy boy!" shouted Basbo. "Basbo pullemout!" He vaulted over the gate, hit the snow and promptly disappeared.

"Where'd Basbo go?" asked Twig.

"I think," said Hooey, looking at the dark hole in the snow,

he went down there.

BOXER SHORTS AND BOBBLE HATS

They all gathered around and peered
solemnly into the hole.

"That doesn't look good," said Twig.
"Although I think it's what he
would have wanted."

"He's not *dead*, Twig," said Hooey. "He's
just fallen down a hole."

"I reckon it's an old tin mine," said Wayne.
"My grandad warned me about them."

"Now you tell us," said Yasmin. "Anything else we should know about, Wayne? Earthquakes? Escaped tigers?"

"We should check he's all right," said Samantha.

"Good idea," said Twig. "But be careful while you're down there – it looks pretty deep."

"I'm not going down there, you big numpty," said Samantha.

"Hold my trousers," said Hooey.

"I'm sorry…?" said Samantha.

"Not you," said Hooey. "I was talking to Twig."

"I don't want to hold your trousers," said
Twig. "I've got enough trouble with my
own, thank you very much."

"Twig, do me a favour. Just shut up and
hold my trousers."

Twig grabbed Hooey's waistband and
Hooey leaned forward until he was looking
down into the centre of the hole.

"Can't see much," he said.

He leaned out a bit further, cupped his hands round his mouth and called, "**Basbo, can you hear me?**"

"Give one knock for yes, and two knocks for no," said Wayne.

"I'll give you three knocks if you don't shut up," said Samantha.

Hooey listened. At first all he could hear was the sound of the wind, but then, very faintly, Basbo's voice floated up through the cold winter air.

"I int bashin' no babbies no more," he said sadly.

I's bashin' me legster and me legster int likin' it.

Suddenly there was a swishing sound and
Will skidded to a halt at the bottom of the
hill. He was strapped into an old armchair
with a wooden door nailed
to the bottom and a
picnic hamper on the
back. Hooey saw
that he had
a half-drunk
cup of coffee
in one hand and
a pad of paper in
the other.
He looked
as if he was
relaxing at
home in front
of the television,
except for the
fact that he was

wearing a scarf and a bobble hat and sitting in the middle of a snowy field.

"You look worried," he said, leaning casually on the parking brake and pushing a small garden spade into the snow.

Is there a problem?

When Hooey had explained the situation, Will frowned and said, "How long's he been down there?"

"About two minutes," said Twig. "Two minutes and three seconds if you count how long it took me to tell you that. And now about two minutes seven sec—"

37

"OK, Twig, we get the picture," said
Hooey. "Maybe one of us should run back
and get help."

"Like Batman, you mean?" said Wayne.

FLAP, FLAP,
HOLD IT RIGHT THERE,
PUNK!

"You do know Batman's not real,
don't you, Wayne?" said Yasmin.

"Shush, shush, *shush*!" said Twig,
clamping his hands over Wayne's ears.
"Don't say things like that, even in fun."

"We'll go, Yasmin," said Samantha. "We've got skis on, so it shouldn't take us long."

"You don't even know where Batman lives," said Wayne.

"He *is* a man of mystery," said Twig.

"We'll manage," said Samantha. "And if Batman's not in we'll just try someone else, like, hmmm, let me think, the emergency services, for example."

"Aaaieeeee, me legster!" shouted Basbo as the girls skied off across the fields. "Me legster's a-moanin' annna groanin annna wanninna go hoamin'!"

"We need to get him out of there," said Hooey. "**Any thoughts, Will?**"

"Loads," said Will. "I just need to make sure I choose the right ones."

"Remember that time you invented a petrol-powered cheese grater?" said Twig. "That was definitely a wrong one."

"Oh, I don't know," said Hooey. "We needed new curtains anyway. These things often have a way of turning out for the best."

"Unless you're stuck down a mineshaft with your leg wrapped round your head," said Wayne.

"What we need is a plan," said Will, "and I reckon I've got a good one."

He took a stick from the picnic hamper and drew an X in the snow.

Now this is us, yes?

Everyone nodded except Wayne, who checked to see if he had turned into a letter of the alphabet without noticing.

"**And this,**" Will continued, drawing a stick figure with a sad face, "**is Basbo.** Now, the first thing we need to know is how far he's fallen."

41

Hooey put a
snowball in Will's
hand and he walked
to the edge of the
hole.

"**Observe**," he
said.

He dropped the
snowball and pressed
the button on his
stopwatch. There
was a little beep,
a "Yaaargh!"
from Basbo and
then another beep
as he pressed his
stopwatch again.

"1.257 seconds," said Will. "By my reckoning that means he's about seven metres down or, to put it another way, three pairs of trousers, three jumpers, three coats and some rope. So come on everyone.

Get your clothes off and let's get this show on the road!

TOURNIQUET TROUSERS

"Isn't your brother going to take his clothes off too?" asked Wayne.

"Of course he isn't," said Hooey.

"Why not?" asked Wayne.

"Because he's a genius, that's why. And geniuses need to keep their brains warm. If Will's brain gets too cold then all his brilliant ideas will freeze and shatter. Is that really what you want, Wayne? **Is it?**"

"No, no, that would be terrible," said Wayne. "Maybe we should tie our coats around his head for extra protection."

"Thank you, but that won't be necessary," said Will.

"Will should be Prime Minister," said Twig. "**Or maybe even Queen.**"

"I want to be a racing driver when I grow up," said Wayne. "Zooming around with sacks full of cash. How about you, Twig?"

"**Top model probably,**" said Twig. "You get to put all those lovely clothes on, and then no one

makes you take them off in the middle of a freezing cold field."

"Quit moaning, Twig," said Hooey, who had already taken off his coat and trousers and was busy unbuttoning his shirt. "The quicker we get our clothes off, the quicker we can rescue Basbo and make sure his leg doesn't fall off."

"**What if it's fallen off already?**" asked Wayne.

"We'll make him a new one," said Twig. "There's loads of trees around. We just need a leggy-shaped branch."

Will cleared his throat and pointed to a new diagram he had drawn.

"Now this is us up here. And this is Basbo down there."

Hooey looked at the diagram and saw that it was a picture of Will on his sledge, heading off down the next hill. Twig and Wayne were standing next to the hole with their arms open, as if they were waiting to catch something. Basbo was sitting at the bottom with a sad expression on his face. And someone else was dangling down the mineshaft from a line of clothes.

"Who's that there?" asked Hooey.

"That would be … you," said Will.

"Tied to a load of old washing? In my boxer shorts?"

"It's not as bad as it looks," said Will. "Soon as you're down there, you tie yourself to Basbo and hang on for dear life."

"Why?" asked Hooey. "What's going to happen?"

"The **SHRIMPTON SUPERSONIC SLEDGE**," replied Will, tapping the side of his armchair. "That's what's going to happen."

They all got to work tying the shirts to the coats and the coats to the trousers until at last there was a long line of clothes stretched across the snow.

"Now," said Will, uncoiling a length of rope from his picnic basket. "This rope isn't long enough, so you need to tie one end to the clothes while I tie the other end to the sledge. Then we're ready to go."

Hooey tied the rope around both legs of his trousers, dragged them to the edge of the hole and peered down into the darkness.

How's it going down there?

he called.

"Pasty annna chips wivva ketchup plizz," Basbo called back.

Annna salty vinger too.

"I think he's hungry," said Hooey.

Wayne rummaged
in his pocket and
pulled out a lump
of toffee with bits
of fluff stuck to it.

"There you go,"
he said. "I was
saving it for an
emergency, but
I can always get
another one."

He threw it down the hole and there
was a faint clunk, followed by an "Orrrf!"
and then the sound of chewing.

Wayne looked at Hooey and nodded.
"Should keep him quiet for a while," he said.

SUPERSONIC SLEDGE

Hooey held the knot on the end of Twig's trousers, stepped over the edge and began walking down the side of the hole. It was a bit slippy at first, but he found that if he bounced away from the wall he could descend more quickly. When he was about halfway down, he looked up and saw the line of clothes stretching away into the circle of light above him.

"'Lo," said a voice beneath his feet. "Avver got fishen chips wivva salty vinger?"

The clothes rope went slack and Hooey landed with a bump on Basbo's leg.

"Arrrrrrrgh, asssa baddy-brokey one!" shouted Basbo, shoving Hooey off and clutching his leg. "Izza makin' me eyes popunn me yed issplode!"

"Sorry about that," said Hooey. "Didn't see you there."

"I's downa hole," said Basbo sadly.

"I's downa hole ann me leg's busty-broken. I's wannin' beeyup inna sun beeyin' a king an bashin' uppa babbies."

Hooey looked at Basbo's leg and guessed the only part he would be playing was the part of a patient in the Accident & Emergency ward. But he just smiled and said, "The first thing we need to do is get you out of here."

"Ow tuvv ear," agreed Basbo, nodding his head.

Ow tuvv ear, yuzz.

"So," Hooey went on, "I'm just going to need to tie a pair of Twig's trousers round your waist."

"I no wearina Twigster's trousicles!" said Basbo.

"You don't have to wear them exactly," said Hooey. "Lift your arms up and I'll show you."

To Hooey's surprise, Basbo lifted his arms up like a toddler waiting to be dressed and Hooey tied the trouser legs in a double knot around his waist.

"Izz vay magic trousers?" asked Basbo.

"In a way, yes," said Hooey.

Basbo closed his eyes and muttered, "Abby ca dabby, abby ca dabby," under his breath.

"How's it going down there?" Twig called.

Is he dead?

"No Twig, he's not dead."

"Are you sure?"

"Twig, zip it and listen. I'm going to tie myself to Basbo and then I'm going to call 'OK, ready!' And when I call 'OK, ready!' that's when you need to give Will the signal."

"Right. Gotcha."

Hooey turned to Basbo. "I think he's got it."

"Skoddit," said Basbo. "Skood."

"Now this is the tricky part," said Hooey. "I'm going to have to hang onto you so we can both be pulled out at the same time."

"Hugsies?" said Basbo, holding out his arms.

"We should probably keep this between ourselves," said Hooey, stepping forward into Basbo's arms. As Basbo wrapped him in a big bear hug, Hooey squeaked, "OK, ready! OK, ready!" very loudly until he heard Twig shout, "Go!" and then he closed his eyes and waited.

At first, nothing happened. All he could hear was Basbo's breathing and the sound of the wind whistling across the top of the mine.

Woss appnin?

grunted Basbo.

"Not much," said Hooey. "I think Twig must have forgo—"

Then there was a distant roar, the clothes stretched tight and Basbo shot up the side of the mine with Hooey hanging on like a limpet in boxer shorts.

"WAAAAAAH!" shouted Hooey.

"YAAAAARG!" shouted Basbo.

They rocketed up into daylight and Hooey
suddenly found himself sitting astride Basbo,
bouncing across the snow behind Will's
sledge. As Twig and Wayne dived out of the
way, Hooey dug his heels in. Twig's trousers
ripped down the middle and they skidded to
a halt in front of a surprised sheep.

"Baaa," said the sheep, staring at Basbo. Basbo nodded.

All right, Twigster?

he said.

Then he fainted.

A PLAN FOR NAN

"It's not your fault that Basbo broke his leg," said Hooey as they walked to school the next morning. "And anyway, I'm sure Troutson can find someone else crazy enough to play the part of King Herod."

"It's not Basbo I'm worried about," said Twig. "I'm worried about my nan."

"I don't remember seeing her down the mine."

"She wasn't down the mine," said Twig. "She's in hospital."

Hooey frowned. "Are you sure you're not getting her mixed up with Basbo?"

"I think I know the difference," said Twig. "And anyway, she's not in for a broken leg. She's having her hip done."

"How come?"

"She was by the fish counter in Sainsbury's when they started playing 'The Macarena' over the tannoy. She got carried away, slipped on a salmon fritter and fell into a pile of tinned peas."

"I thought vegetables were supposed to be good for you," said Hooey. "But they'll look after her in hospital, won't they?"

"Maybe, but it means she won't get
to see me in the school play. It's all she's
talked about since I got the part of **LEAD
SHEEP** and now she's going to miss it."

"Maybe we could set up some kind
of satellite link, like they do for the
Eurovision Song Contest," said Hooey.

"**Ooh,** we could all dress up!" cried Twig,
clapping his hands together.

"Twig, it's a Christmas play," said Hooey.
"We'll be dressed up already."

"Even better," said Twig. He put his hand
in his pocket and pulled out fifty pence.

"How much
do you think
a satellite link
will cost?"

"More than
that," said
Hooey.

"No point keeping it then," said Twig, pushing open the door of the sweetshop.

Mr Danson was putting the finishing touches to his winter window display.

"**Hello, boys!**" he said as the doorbell dinged. "Welcome to my **Winter Wonderland of Marshmallow Mountains and Sherbety Snowstorms!**"

He smiled and pointed to a sky made from pink candyfloss. Below it, liquorice people played with sherbet snowmen and jelly babies skied down marshmallow hills.

"I'd *love* to live there," said Twig. "Imagine if everything around you tasted of sweets."

"In my shop, everything does!" cried Mr Danson,

pointing at the chocolate counter and the shelves full of colourful jars. "So what would you like from my world today, boys?"

"Have you got any satellite links?" asked Twig.

Mr Danson scratched his head. "Have they got sherbet in them?"

"I don't think so."

"Then, no," said Mr Danson. "I could do you a bag of flying saucers?"

"Done," said Twig. "Can I have 50p's worth, please?"

Mr Danson
pushed the bag
of sweets across the
counter then leaned over to
Hooey and whispered, "I know this is not
a confectionery-related enquiry, but why
does your friend need a satellite link?"

"So his nan can watch him in the
Christmas play," said Hooey. "The trouble
is, she's stuck in hospital, so she can't come
and see it."

"Forgive me for stating the obvious," said
Mr Danson, "but if she can't go to the play,
would it not be easier to take the play to her?"

* * *

"The main problem," said Will, "is actually getting into the hospital."

"Don't they have **doors** like in the olden days?" asked Twig.

"They do," said Will, "but they also have **Nurse Maloney**. Nurse Maloney does not like **visitors** and she does not like **noise**. In fact, there is only one thing that Nurse Maloney hates more than **visitors** and **noise**."

"What's that?" asked Twig.

"**Children**," said Hooey. "Will went down and checked the place out, didn't you Will?"

"I did," said Will. "I told Nurse Maloney that we were interested in performing a Christmas play for the patients and asked her what she thought would be most convenient. She said what would be most convenient would be if I went away and took a long walk off a short pier. She said that children were not allowed into her ward unless they'd had a terrible accident and that, if I carried on bothering her, it was something she could certainly arrange."

"She sounds lovely," said Twig.

"If by lovely you mean **stark staring bug-eyed crazy** then, yes, she was very lovely indeed," said Will.

"So that's it then," said
Twig, pressing his hand
against his forehead.
"My nan will never
see me perform."

"Unless…" said Hooey.

"Unless what?"

"Unless you're
an adult."

"I'm not sure I'll still
remember my lines by then," said Twig.

"I don't mean an actual adult," said Hooey.
"I mean you dress up as an adult to throw
Maloney off the scent
while we get your scene
started. Then while she's
distracted you come
in, do your bit and,
hooray for Twig,
everyone's happy."

Twig's eyes widened with excitement. "I could dress up as a **nurse!** Wait… I could dress up as **a sheep and a nurse!**"

"I'm not sure," said Hooey. "Do you really think you can pull it off?"

"Of *course* I can pull it off!" cried Twig, clapping his hands and skipping round in circles.

TWIG IN TIGHTS

"These Spanxy tights are well comfy," said Twig, tottering around in the high heels Hooey had found at the back of his mum's wardrobe. "70 **Denier with a Matt Finish and Reinforced Gusset.** None of your rubbish."

"Forget the tights," said Hooey, "It's your bra that needs sorting out."

"Um, hello?" said Twig. "We're talking about a **Lacy Lucy** here, with **flowery detail and full under-wiring.**"

"Yeah, but you've got it on back to front, you big doughnut," said Will. "Come here."

Excuse me, young man!

said Twig, slapping Will's hands away as he tried to pull the bra round to the front. "Is that any way to treat a lady?"

Will sighed. "He's going to be like this all day, isn't he?"

"Just warming up," said Hooey.

Twig pulled out a little black brush and smeared mascara across his eyelashes.

Hooey grinned. "Looking good, girlfriend."

"Maybe we should go through the plan again," said Will. He picked up a ruler and tapped the front of his flip chart. "OK, Twig. Stop looking in the mirror and pay attention."

"Hang on while I smudge my smoky kitten eyes."

Twig's cousin Sandra had lent him her spare nurse's uniform and Hooey had to admit that, along with the ginger wig, Twig really looked the part.

"I think you need more blusher," said Hooey, dabbing at Twig's cheeks. "Brings out your natural colour."

"Whenever you girls are ready," said Will.
Hooey coughed, put the blusher down
and folded his arms. "**Sorry.** Got a bit
carried away there."

"Twig?"

Twig sat on the bed
with his legs crossed,
tucked a few strands of
hair behind his ears and
fluttered his eyelashes.
"OK," he said.
"I'm ready for
some serious
nursin'."

* * *

The wall by the hospital car park was less
than a metre high, but it was tall enough to
hide Will, Hooey, Nurse Twig, Yasmin and
Ricky the Sheep.

"*I feel stupid,*" said Ricky.

"*That's because you are stupid,*"
said Yasmin.

"No, it's because I'm in a **car park** dressed as a **sheep**," said Ricky. "Where are the other sheep anyway?"

"Well, one's disguised as a nurse and the others should follow along any minute," said Hooey, checking his watch. "You know what sheep are like."

"Here they come," said Yasmin, peering over the wall. "And they've got their shepherds with them."

The three shepherds all wore dressing
gowns and tea towels on their heads. Two
were Frank and Freddie Frinton and the third
was Sarah-Jane Silverton. Their sheep were
Wayne and Marty, who were both wearing
cardboard ears and white woolly jumpers.

"Evening, all," said Freddie, waving his shepherd's crook.

Anyone need anything rounding up?

"I didn't know you were a shepherd, Sarah-Jane," said Yasmin.

"I'm still going to be **Mary** in the school play," said Sarah-Jane. "But when I heard you were doing the shepherd scene, I thought you might need someone with **dramatic experience.**"

"We're going to have a dramatic experience right here in the car park if you don't keep your voice down," said Will.

"Where's Samantha?" asked Ricky.

"She wasn't in when I called round for her," said Yasmin. "I think she might be getting her hair done."

"But that means we haven't got an Angel Gabriel," said Ricky.

"What?" asked Twig, checking his make-up in the mirror of a Ford Fiesta.

"Nothing to worry about, Twig," said Hooey, then turned to Will. *"We haven't got an Angel Gabriel!"* he whispered.

"Leave it with me," said Will, writing **"Replacement Angel"** in his notebook. "OK, good folk of Bethlehem, it's 7p.m. and we need to get this show on the road. Twig, Hooey, you know what to do. We'll wait here until you give the signal and then we'll move in."

"Break a leg, everyone," said Hooey. "Except for Basbo, of course."

He linked arms
with Twig and
together they walked
towards the hospital entrance, Twig's high
heels clacking noisily across the tarmac.

"That is one classy
looking nurse," said
Wayne. "Is she a
new girl?"

* * *

"Seems like a nice relaxing place," said Twig when they reached the main reception area. It was full of people milling around and sitting on plastic chairs, drinking coffee. "Maybe we should fall over and break something. **Have ourselves a holiday.**"

"This is no time to be thinking about holidays, Twig," said Hooey. "You need to be thinking about what you're going to say to Nurse Maloney. "Cos if you mess up, this is going to be the least relaxing place on the planet."

"Great," said Twig. "**No pressure, then.**"

The lift doors opened and Hooey pressed the button for the third floor.

"OK, Twig, get ready," he said. "**You and me are going all the way to Nurseville.**"

MAD MALONEY

"Do you think that's her?" asked Twig as
they peered round the corner.

A tall, thick-set woman stood next to
the nurses' station with her arms folded.

"Yup, that's her all right," said Hooey.
The woman's sleeves were rolled up and,
even from this distance, Hooey could make
out the skull and crossbones tattooed on
her muscly forearm.

"Maybe she's a pirate," said Twig.

"She's wearing a nurse's uniform," said Hooey.

"So am I," said Twig. "Doesn't make me a nurse."

"Well, for the next ten minutes you'd better make sure it does," said Hooey. "Otherwise we're going to find ourselves walking the plank out of a top-floor window."

Twig pulled out a compact mirror, checked his mascara and smacked his lips together.

"Hello, Nurse Twiggy, you little fox," he said.

"Just go," said Hooey. "Go, go, GO."

As Twig tottered up the corridor towards
Nurse Maloney, Hooey's phone buzzed.
Will's name was on the display.

How's it
going, Will?

he whispered.

"I'm in a car park with three sheep, two shepherds and a barmaid," said Will. "People are getting suspicious. We definitely need to move out ASAP."

"*Twig should be on target in about five seconds,*" said Hooey. "*Once he's there we'll be in a can-do, green-light situation. Can you hold out until then?*"

"OK, but we're still short of an angel," said Will. "Any potentials up there with you?"

Hooey watched Nurse Maloney scowl at Twig as he teetered down the corridor in his high heels.

"Definitely none up here," he said. "You're going to have to improvise."

"Why, hel-lo," said Twig in a sing-songy voice. "You must be Nurse Maloney, am I right?" He lightly tapped the end of her nose with his finger. "I can tell it's you by that naughty, *naughty* smile!"

Nurse Maloney wasn't smiling. She looked like a Dobermann that had just been told dinner was cancelled.

Touch me again and you'll wake up in A&E,

she said in a voice that sounded like a washing machine full of gravel.

"Oh, stop it, you!" said Twig with a girlish giggle. **"I'm already in stitches!"**

Hooey put his hands over his eyes.

"Enough of this nonsense," said Nurse Maloney. "Who are you and what do you want?"

"I," said Twig, putting on a serious face, "am part of the new inspection team. We're here to make sure standards of hygiene and cleanliness are up to scratch."

"I haven't heard anything about this," said Nurse Maloney.

"Of course you haven't," said Twig. "If I'd told you I was coming you'd have been bustling about with your little squeegee mop, trying to **pull the wool over my eyes.**"

"I can assure you—"

"Can you, though?" said Twig, running his finger along the top of the reception counter and examining it. "I mean, **Hello, people.** Ring, ring, Earth calling Nurse Maloney. What do we have here?" He showed her the tip of his finger. "**Is it DUST?**" He stared at her and nodded his head slowly up and down. "**I THINK IT IS!**"

"Well, I can assure you, Miss, um, Miss…"

"Twiggy."

"I can assure you, Miss Twiggy, that I take hygiene very seriously here in my ward."

"Oh, it's *your* ward, is it?"

"Yes. It is."

"Right. Well done. Just testing."

Hooey could tell that Twig was starting to enjoy his new role as hospital inspector just a little bit too much. He was definitely talking rubbish now. From the way Nurse Maloney was staring at him, she clearly thought so too.

Excuse me,

Hooey said, walking down the corridor. "Are you the hospital inspector who was on our ward earlier?"

"Why, yes, that was me, dear," said Twig, looking relieved. "How can I help?"

"Well," said Hooey, "I just wanted to say before I go home that when you said the children's ward was the cleanest ward you had ever seen, you obviously didn't see some of the things I saw."

"I didn't?" said Twig.

"No, you did not," said Hooey. "There's dirt all over the place up there."

"Of course there is!" cried Nurse Maloney triumphantly.

Those dirty, filthy children!

"And as for this ward, I wish I'd stayed here to be honest," Hooey went on. "It's so clean, it's like standing in the middle of a dishwasher."

"What, with a load of dirty plates?" asked Twig.

"No, you know, one that's come to the end of its cycle."

Twig looked confused. "Like Bradley Wiggins?"

"What he means, Nurse Twiggy," said Nurse Maloney, "is that my ward is the cleanest, brightest ward in the whole hospital." She turned to Hooey and smiled. "You are very smart for a child," she said. "Are you sure you're not a grown-up?"

"Quite sure," said Hooey. "But I can see from Nurse Twiggy's face that she doesn't believe me."

"I do actually," said Twig.

"No, you don't."

"I do."

"**No, you don't,**" Hooey said hurriedly. "Which is why I think it's important that Nurse Maloney comes up to the children's ward to see for herself."

"**Oh, right, yeah. Got it,**" said Twig, putting his thumbs up behind Nurse Maloney's back.

"I think that is an excellent idea!" said Nurse Maloney. "We'll soon see who has and who hasn't got the cleanest ward around here!"

As they marched back along the corridor, Hooey's phone rang.

"Hello? Yes, we're just going to see how dirty the children's ward is."

"What?" said Will on the other end of the phone.

"Who is this and what have you done with my brother?"

"It's me," said Hooey. "I'm just telling you I'm **TAKING NURSE MALONEY TO THE CHILDREN'S WARD.** Which means that **NURSE MALONEY WILL NOT BE AT HER STATION.** We have a **GREEN-LIGHT SITUATION,** if you **UNDERSTAND** what I'm **SAYING.**"

"Message received and understood," said Will. "OK, sheep and shepherds, go! Barmaid, go! Let's do this, people! Hooey, see you in five!"

"We'd better hurry up," said Hooey, putting the phone back in his pocket. "Seems like the flock is on the move."

Nurse Maloney stared at him suspiciously. "Who was that?"

Hooey thought quickly. "**Some crazy farmer,**" he said. "On about sheep and stuff. Probably a wrong number."

As Nurse Maloney punched her way through some double doors, Hooey wondered what she would do if she knew that she was being followed by a boy dressed in nurse's uniform who would soon be dancing around her ward in a sheep costume.

Then he thought:

Probably best not to think about it.

LAMB LAMBADA

The children's ward was another five floors up and by the time they got there, Nurse Maloney had counted off on her fingers the three reasons why she didn't like children.

"One: They're noisy.

Two: They're smelly.

Three: They're noisy and smelly."

"That's four reasons," said Twig.

"Two actually," said Hooey. Nurse Maloney glared at him and he added, "But who's counting?"

"Here we are, the children's ward," said Twig, walking up to the young nurse standing in the doorway. "Hello, Nurse Twiggy here. We've just come to see how filthy your ward is."

"I beg your pardon?" said the nurse.

"Apology accepted," said Twig. "Well, it was very nice meeting you. Bye!"

"Just you hold on there a minute, Nurse Twiggy," said Nurse Maloney, grabbing Twig by the arm. "I think you've got some explaining to do."

"Ah," said Twig as both nurses put their hands on their hips and stared at him.

Issa nursicle nightmare, issa a nursicle nightmare!

shouted a voice from the other end of the ward.

Izza Twigster nursey-man annee dressin-in disguisey-woo!

A large, shaven-headed boy with his leg in plaster was sitting up in bed and pointing at Twig in horror.

> Nursey-boy cummin-in disguisey-woo! Nursey-boy disguisely-woo gonna frow me downa mine!

"It's Basbo," whispered Hooey. "He's recognized you."

"In *this* outfit?" said Twig. "I don't think so."

"Nursey-Twig gonna get fruitna-hed," growled Basbo, grabbing an apple from the fruit bowl on his bedside table.

"What's fruitna-hed?" asked Twig.

Basbo threw the apple and it struck Twig's forehead like a bullet, knocking him flat on his back.

"OK, got it," he said, sitting up and wiping apple pips from his eyes. "*Fruit* in the *head.*"

"*Twig!*" hissed Hooey, tapping the top of his own head.

Twig frowned,
then turned to see
Nurse Maloney
staring at him with
raised eyebrows.
Twig put his hands on his head and then
glanced at the floor where his wig was lying
next to the tea trolley like a ginger wombat.

"**Uh-oh,**" he said.

"You're … you're … you're not a hospital
inspector at all!"
gasped Nurse
Maloney,
shaking an
accusing
finger at
him. "You're,
you're … **a boy!**"

"No, I'm not,"
shouted Twig, ripping
off his nurse's uniform to reveal
cardboard ears and a white woolly
jumper. "I'm a sheep!"

"Issa Twig inna sheep inna
nursey-fing!" cried Basbo. "Izza-
enndovva world!"

"Go for it, Twig!" shouted Hooey as Basbo
leapt out of bed and fell flat on his face.
"Give 'em a sheep-show to remember!"

"Baa!" shouted Twig, bursting out
through the double doors. "Baa, baa,
baaaaaaah!"

"Ooh, he's good," said a young nurse wistfully, watching Twig disappear off down the corridor. "For a moment I was back on Daddy's farm there, standing in a field and listening to—"

"Snap out of it, Nurse!" said Nurse Maloney, clapping her hands in front of her eyes. "There's a **Sheep Boy** loose in my hospital and I'm not going to stand for it, do you hear? We're going to get out there and we're going to hunt him down like the dirty dog he is."

"I think you mean **sheep**," said Hooey. "Dirty sheep."

"Shut up," snapped the nurse. "**Shut up, shut up, SHUT UP!**"

Hooey glanced over
at Basbo and noticed that:
a) he was sliding back across the floor,
b) there was now a rope attached to his
waist and c) Will was behind the bed,
pulling on the other end of it.

Hooey mouthed, "What are you doing?"
but Will just disappeared behind the bed
again. Hooey turned and ran towards the
lift. Hearing Nurse Maloney pounding
down the corridor behind him, he pointed
upwards, shouted, "Sheep Boy went
that way!" and raced down the stairs,
three at a time. As he stopped to catch
his breath, he heard the sound of children

singing "While Shepherds Watched" and
realized that at least some of the cast must
have reached their target.

"Hooey!" hissed a voice. *"Is that you?"*

Hooey turned to see a pair of cardboard
sheep's ears sticking out from
behind the door
of the staff toilet.

"Twig, what are
you doing?" Hooey
hissed back.

"I caught my woolly jumper in
the lift door," said Twig. "It sort of …
unravelled."

The door swung open to reveal Twig wrapped in several rolls of white toilet paper.

"This was the next best thing," he said. "What d'you think?"

"Bit weird," said Hooey. "You look like a mummified sheep."

"Still a sheep though, right?"

"If I narrow my eyes a bit," said Hooey. "Then narrow them a bit more until they're

closed. Now, get in there and start bleating
before Nurse Maloney puts lamb chop on
the hospital menu."

Twig grinned. "Take me to your sheep,
Bo Peep," he said, dancing out of the toilet
and into the corridor.

Let's put the lamb in this lambada!

A SPECIAL SURPRISE

When they reached the ward, Sarah-Jane
was playing "Sheep May Safely Graze" on
a small accordion while Freddie, Frank
and Marty snuffled around on the floor
making sheep noises. Twig's nan sat up in
bed watching with her hands clasped to her
chest while the other ladies on the ward
gathered around her to watch.

"Which one's your grandson?" asked the lady with a blue-rinse.

"That one, I think," said Twig's nan, pointing at Sarah-Jane Silverton. "I never knew he could play the flute."

"I think it's an accordion," whispered the lady opposite.

"That can't be right," said Twig's Nan. "Sheep can't play accordions."

"**Baaaa!**" cried Twig, suddenly remembering his lines and skidding into the middle of the room. He threw his arms open and said softly:

We are the sheep,
Who sing while you sleep,
On a mountain so steep,
Of a secret so deep.
And the shepherds all keep
Careful watch of their ...
umm ... sheep."

For a moment, all was quiet and Hooey saw Twig's nan gazing out of the window at the stars. Then two of the shepherds stepped forward and began speaking.

"Cold tonight, Nathan."

"Aye."

"Very cold in fact."

"Aye."

"Freezing in fact."

"Aye."

"Aye, aye, you two,".
said the third shepherd.
"Cold tonight, isn't it?"

"Aye."

Then, as Yasmin began
playing "While Shepherds
Watched" again on her recorder, all the
sheep leaned forward and lifted
up their ears.

"That's nice," said Shepherd
Wayne. "What is it, Barmaid?"

"Just a little tune I've
been working on," said
Yasmin. "What are you
lot up to, anyway?"

"Watching our flocks mostly," said Frank.
"They've been quite frisky this evening."

Twig the Sheep turned to Ricky the Sheep
and said:

"Cold tonight, isn't it?"

"Aye."

The sheep all looked at the shepherds.

Twig said, "I wish I had a nice warm coat like them. I wonder where they got them from."

"Remember that time in the summer when they jumped on us?"

"Aye."

"And there was that clickety-clacking sound and all of a sudden it was nice and cool?"

"Aye."

Well, that's where they got their coats from.

Hooey saw that
Twig's nan was
smiling. Under
the cardboard
ears and the
many layers of
toilet roll, Twig
was smiling too.

"WAIT!" said Twig, pointing towards the
door. "What IS that incredible sight I see
approaching?"

Everyone looked towards the door, but
there was nothing to be seen except an old
mop and a tea trolley.

"Wait!" Twig repeated, still pointing at
the door. "What is that incredible
sight I see approaching?"

As the lady with the blue-rinsed hair
coughed awkwardly into the silence, Hooey
realized that Twig was waiting for the Angel

124

Gabriel to appear. But the Angel Gabriel was Samantha, and Samantha wasn't coming. Unfortunately, no one had thought to tell Twig.

Twig stood up, cupped his hands around his mouth and shouted:

There was a loud gasp from the audience
and, just for a moment, Hooey thought
that Samantha had made it after all. But
then he saw that no one was looking at
the doorway; they were all staring in the
other direction. And the reason they were
all staring in the other direction was that a
large, shaven-headed boy in a white sheet

 was dangling
outside the
window on the
end of a thick
rope. One of
his legs was in
plaster and kept
bumping against
the glass, but
he seemed
quite cheerful
and somehow

even managed to raise his arms level with his head. He appeared to be shouting something, but no one could hear him because the window was closed.

"Sheep Boy's not wrong," said Ricky. "That IS an incredible sight."

As Freddie jumped up to open the window, Basbo swung into the ward with his plastered leg stuck out in front of him and his white sheet billowing backwards in the cold night air.

> **I izz bringinnoo va tidings ovva great joy,**

he said, flapping his arms like wings. He swung in and out of the window several times before Yasmin and Ricky managed to catch hold of him, lowering him to the floor with a bump.

"**Izza gonnbeeya babby,**" he said. "**A special babby izzonnizz way.**"

As all the ladies *oooh*ed and *ahh*ed, Hooey remembered that Will was upstairs on the other end of the rope. But as he reached for his phone, the doors flew open and Nurse Maloney stood in the doorway, her face purple with rage.

"**SO!**" she shouted. "I have found you at last, **you horrible children**! I have tracked you down, and now every last one of you will pay the price, **do you understand?**"

"Aye," whimpered the sheep.

"Aye," whimpered the shepherds.

"Hooray!" shouted the ladies. "Three cheers for Nurse Maloney!"

"Eh?" said Hooey.

"Weez allovuss swappin'!" said Basbo happily.

"Weez allovuss swappinna parts!"

"**Eh?**" said Nurse Maloney.

"That was marvellous, dear," Twig's nan said to her. "The way you pretended to hate those children, I think it's quite the best King Herod I've ever seen!"

KILL VA BABBIES!

shouted Basbo, hobbling over to Nurse Maloney and putting his arms around her. "You izza good acty-person, Missus Nursey-Man."

"I am?" said Nurse Maloney and Hooey thought he saw the hint of a smile cross her lips.

"My dear, sweet boy!" said Twig's nan as Twig did a sheep-like shuffle around her bed. "You went to all this trouble just for me?"

But Twig just walked to the window and stared out into the darkness.

"You did it, Twig!" Hooey said. "Everyone loved it!"

"They did, didn't they?" said Twig.

They were quiet for a few moments. Then Twig said, "I really thought Samantha would come. But she didn't."

"I'm sure she would have done," said Hooey. He patted Twig on the shoulder. "I expect life just got in the way, that's all."

They were picking up the last strands
of toilet roll that had come undone during
Twig's lambada, when the ward doors
opened and a small figure walked in
carrying a knitted blanket.

"Who's that?"
asked Wayne.
"It's Samantha,"
said Twig.

Samantha smiled.
"Hello everyone," she
said. "I just came to
apologize for not
making it on time."

"We don't need an angel any more," said Ricky. "**We've got Basbo.**"

"Well, that's good," said Samantha. "But I just wanted to explain. You see, the thing is, my sister got rushed into hospital unexpectedly."

"Oh, no," said Twig's nan. "I'm so sorry."

"Don't be sorry," said Samantha. "It's a good thing."

Ricky frowned. "Why? Don't you like her?"

"**Of course I like her,**" said Samantha. "But when I told her that I'd missed your Christmas play, she said I could bring something else along to make up for it."

She walked slowly across the ward and sat down in the armchair next to Twig's nan.

And as the old ladies and nurses and shepherds and sheep and barmaid and Basbo all gathered around, Samantha smiled, and pushed back the blanket, and showed them exactly what that something else was.

"I wazza tellin' youz wazzen-eye?" said Basbo with a big grin on his face. "I wazza tellin' youz! Izza gonnbeeya babby. A special babby izzonnizz way!"

BRIGHT LIGHTS AND LOONS

"I expect you must have had to do an awful lot of safety checks before you let Basbo down on that rope," said Sarah-Jane as they all walked out beneath the stars.

"Not really," said Will. "I just tied it round his waist with a couple of granny knots and asked him if he felt OK. He said, 'Yarse' and then I pushed him out the window."

"I think he liked being an angel,"
said Hooey.

They watched a squirrel run
across the car park and up into a
tree.

"My Uncle Dave says you're
never more than thirty centimetres
away from a squirrel," said Wayne.

"Yeah, but your Uncle Dave lives in a
caravan," said Twig. "In the woods."

Wayne nodded. "It's got a toilet and
everything."

"Living the dream, eh, Wayne?" said
Yasmin.

"It was like a dream today really," said
Twig. "What with me dressed up as a nurse,
Basbo flying about on a rope and a load of
sheep singing to a bunch of old ladies. It's
the kind of dream I usually only get after
eating too much cheese."

"But it wasn't a dream, was it?" said Will. "And you know why?" He took out his notebook and tapped it with his pencil. "Careful planning, that's why."

Hooey thought for a moment. "Will's right," he said. "None of that would have happened if we hadn't had the bonkers idea in the first place. And it may interest you to know that I have actually, just this second, come up with **another brilliant plan**."

He lowered his voice to a whisper and beckoned everyone closer.

"You have to listen carefully," he said.

I don't want to say it too loudly, in case someone overhears.

As everyone gathered around expectantly, Hooey waited a second or two.

Then he smiled, took a deep breath and shouted:

LAST ONE TO THE SWEET SHOP'S A CRAZY-FACED LOON!

For a moment, there was stunned silence.
Then, as they all squeaked and squealed
and chased after him, Hooey ran past the
park and the beach huts and the tumbling
sea, listening to the crash of the waves and
the sound of laughter mixed up with his
breath, and he kept on running, running
and running until at last Twig caught up
with him, wheezing and giggling and
crossing his legs.

SHWEET!

he shouted,
holding up both
hands for Hooey
to high-five...

"...SHWEET, SHWEET, SHERWEET-SHOP, SHER-WEET!"

Then, still laughing, they all linked arms and ran away through the dark, empty streets to the bright shining lights of the town.

STEVE VOAKE (also author of the Daisy Dawson series) was born in Midsomer Norton where he spent many years falling off walls, bikes and go-karts before he got older and realized he didn't bounce like he used to. When he was Headteacher of Kilmersdon School he tried to convince children that falling off walls, bikes and go-karts wasn't such a good idea, but no one really believed him. He now enjoys writing the Hooey Higgins stories and hasn't fallen off anything for over a week.

EMMA DODSON has always been inspired by silly stories and loves drawing scruffy little animals and children. She sometimes writes and illustrates her own silly stories – including *Badly Drawn Dog* and *Speckle the Spider*. As well as drawing and painting, Emma makes disgusting things for film and TV. If you've ever seen anyone on telly get a bucket of poo thrown on them or step in a pile of sick you can be fairly sure that she was responsible for making it. Emma also teaches Illustration at the University of Westminster where she gets to talk about more sensible things.